TOO MANY ACORNS

SUSANNAH CRISPE

For my curious collector Jeremy — keep on collecting (but *please* empty your pockets before laundry day ...).
— S.C.

First published 2024

EK Books
an imprint of Exisle Publishing Pty Ltd
PO Box 864, Chatswood, NSW 2057, Australia
226 High Street, Dunedin, 9016, New Zealand
www.ekbooks.org

Copyright © 2024 in text and illustrations: Susannah Crispe

Susannah Crispe asserts the moral right to be identified as the creator of this work.

All rights reserved. Except for short extracts for the purpose of review, no part of this book may be reproduced, stored in a retrieval system or transmitted in any form or by any means, whether electronic, mechanical, photocopying, recording or otherwise, without prior written permission from the publisher.

A CiP record for this book is available from the National Library of Australia.

ISBN 978-1-922539-74-8

Designed by Mark Thacker
Typeset in Aleo regular 17 on 24pt
Printed in China

This book uses paper sourced under ISO 14001 guidelines from well-managed forests and other controlled sources.

10 9 8 7 6 5 4 3 2 1

One quiet day, an acorn dropped at Patrick's feet.

Patrick held the acorn.

It was warm and smooth in his hand.

The acorn was so small, hardly a thing at all.

Picking up another, Patrick felt something inside him grow.

With every acorn, the feeling built.

And built.

He could not stop now.

No one understood that this thing had swept him up, gathering pace, and leaving room for nothing else.

He could not seem to say *This is enough.*

So, on it went, with another acorn.

And another.

Until suddenly there were acorns everywhere he looked.

This had become bigger than him.

Soon, Patrick could no longer find the things that made his heart smile.

Perhaps this will do? he wondered quietly.

The acorns were affecting everyone and everything.

Patrick was beginning to think he might even have too many acorns, when ...

... a groan escaped the house.

Suddenly, the acorns were cascading towards him.

An enormous avalanche, spilling from every room, collecting everything in its path.

Patrick's chin quivered. Dad scowled.

In the silence, another acorn dropped.

And then ...

Dad laughed.
And Patrick laughed.
Just like that, the world seemed a little brighter.

As they swept up the acorns, they talked, and they hugged, and they made a plan.

Together, they found a place for Patrick's acorn. They tended it, and they waited.

Patrick's heart remembered how to smile.

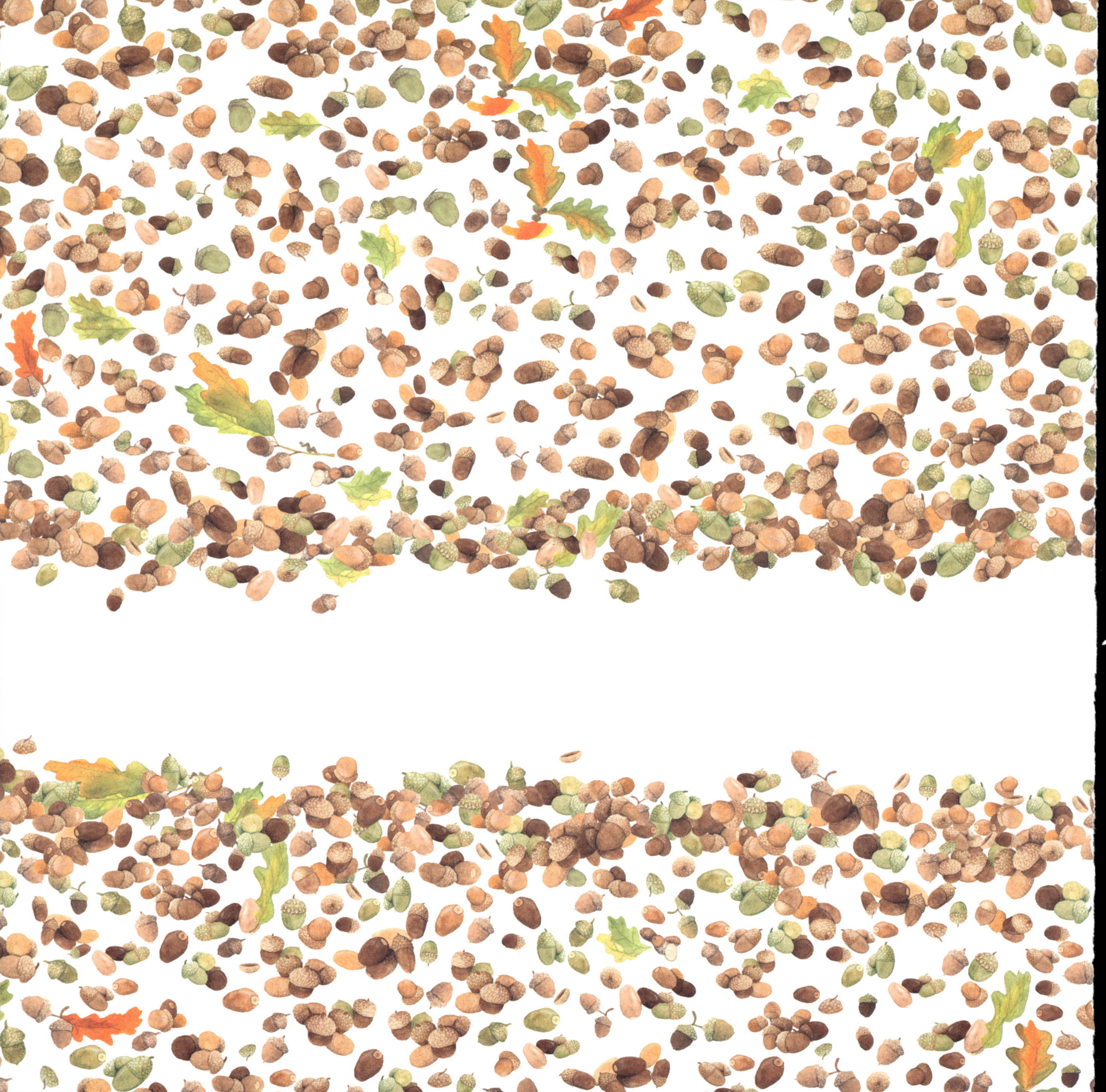